THE HOPE OF
SORROWS

SHORT STORIES OF
THE ALTERED SERIES

JACQUELINE BROWN

Cover art designed by Aero Gallerie

<u>Also by Jacqueline Brown</u>
The Light, Book One of The Light Series
Through the Ashes, Book Two of The Light Series
From the Shadows, Book Three of The Light Series
Into the Embers, Book Four of The Light Series
Out of the Darkness, Book Five of The Light Series
"Before the Silence," a Light Series Short Story

Awakening, Book One of the Awakening Trilogy
Gifted, Book Two of the Awakening Trilogy
Haunted, Book Three of the Awakening Trilogy

Altered, Book One

Please visit the author at www.Jacqueline-Brown.com
for updates, special offers, and new releases.

This work is dedicated to all who strive to make the
world better
~ may you be continuously guided by the Holy Spirit.

Purity of Intention

The young woman was striking both in her physical beauty and in the contempt in her expression. She sat, chin resting on drawn-up knees, in the shade of a sprawling live oak. Loose, faded denim jeans sagged from her legs. Her long, slender arms circled her legs. Her back was bare—except for the thin string preventing the front of her shirt from falling too far from her body. Her skin, brown by nature, had been tinted slightly darker by the harsh Florida sun.

The woman was staring across a weed-covered meadow, at an old stone church. Some of the weeds had grown tall and were starting to flower, creating the impression of more beauty than was actually there. The church was the opposite. Much of the stone was darkened by mold and some chunks had fallen away from the walls, creating the impression of far less beauty than was there.

The physical deterioration was typical for such buildings … outdated, rarely used. The woman, Bakhita, was familiar with the crumbling building. After her family had moved to this town, she was forced to visit it often.

Her parents had been part of a superstitious group who believed, not in science, but in religion. Thankfully, she had escaped their faulty beliefs. They were so different from her, she was astonished how she could be genetically related to either of them. Her parents were not stupid; in fact, they were quite brilliant. However, they didn't value the same sort of knowledge she did and so in her mind this made them foolish.

Bakhita and her brother had received what was considered a classical education by her parents: one steeped in ancient history, philosophy, and literature. The siblings had learned the sciences, of course, but not at the level she would've preferred.

Not until college was she finally able to focus on genetics. This was her gift, the area in which she easily surpassed all those around her. She met Josiah in her first genetics class. She didn't believe in fate, but if she did she would've said fate brought them together. They were the youngest in the class, and excelled at a rate no one, including the professors, could keep up with. Neither of them stayed at the university long. What was the point, when they were already more advanced than every professor at the school?

The wind sent a swift shiver through her body. How anyone, especially Josiah, could ever willingly go into the falling-down church was beyond her. It had always felt uncomfortable to her, as if the silence of the stones caused her pain. Some would say it was her soul crying out for the true, the good, and the beautiful. Bakhita would not have phrased it that way. She was familiar with the term *soul*, of course, having been raised by parents who believed such nonsense. Such a belief was nothing more than a superstitious holdover from ancient times.

It embarrassed her that her parents held such beliefs. Despite this, Bakhita could acknowledge the kindness of her parents; they clearly loved her, her brother, and each other. Overall, she was grateful for them and for her upbringing. After all, if she had not been brought up with what she believed was a full understanding of the old traditions, she may have felt some level of appeal for them or at least been curious. As it was, she had easily walked away from the nonsense as soon as she moved out of her parents' house. In actuality, she understood little of what the ancient traditions entailed, and what portion she did understand she lacked the depth of awareness to fully grasp. A person cannot understand what they aren't aware of, especially if they believe themselves superior to whatever it might be.

On this day in early October, she found herself frustrated that the local government had not already taken over this church so a useful group could utilize the stone structure. For her part, she didn't get involved in politics. Josiah played that role. It was ironic, in a disturbing way: he was now one of the people inside the crumbling building.

He had not chosen to be there, she was sure. He was there because of the other person Bakhita knew was inside. That person and her family were some of those who had fought hardest against allowing the building to be converted to anything useful. How strange: the two of them in the building together. How strange all of this was. How any of it had happened, she couldn't comprehend. She'd spent most of the past month trying to understand, searching her memory for clues, but found none.

Amelia Barnes—the woman who did not want the building used for anything else—was inside getting married. Bakhita scoffed at the words "getting married." What an antiquated term. Typical for Amelia: antiquated, out of touch. How could Josiah Northup possibly be the one she was marrying?

Bakhita was confused as well as infuriated. Josiah had been Bakhita's. In many ways he still was hers. He was her equal in nearly every respect, and they spent almost every moment together—every moment that he was not with Amelia. Bakhita's face contorted at the thought.

Josiah had been her partner first, not in romance, but in business. Together they were shaping the future of their region, and from there … the world. That sounded like a lofty statement; in truth, it downplayed the significance they were having on the world. Bakhita's work in genetic alterations and Josiah's on artificial wombs outpaced every other research team on the planet. Their success stemmed not only from how brilliant each was individually, but also how their minds worked in unison. It was a remarkable partnership. And now he was marrying, actually *marrying* Amelia.

Bakhita stared at the brick path leading from the church into the well-manicured swath of forest near it. She audibly exhaled. She had to believe their work would continue unimpaired, like he'd promised. Josiah was clearly good at keeping his work and private life separate. She, more than anyone, could testify to that. It was the reason she hadn't known he was seeing Amelia until the wedding was a month away.

What was most confusing about this was how, of all the women in the world, he chose Amelia. What had Amelia done to win him? He was a brilliant visionary and she was … well, not even close. She had good qualities; Bakhita was not so biased as to not give her the credit due. Amelia was kind and she seemed to truly care for Josiah. She wasn't ugly or overly stupid, but she was nowhere near the scientist that Bakhita and Josiah were, and she was foolishly superstitious. Bakhita couldn't imagine what Josiah and Amelia spoke about. They had nothing in common. Furthermore, Bakhita had never believed Josiah would agree to marry anyone. It was such an old-fashioned practice. She assumed one day Josiah would partner with someone and, if she was being honest, she always thought, or hoped, it would be her. But marriage? Not in a thousand millennia would she have predicted he'd get married, and certainly not to Amelia Barnes.

"I thought you'd be here," a man said, appearing out of the wooded park behind her.

Bakhita jumped at the sound of his voice. She'd expected to be alone in her contemptuous thoughts. She did not expect her brother to show up.

"Are you here to gloat?" Bakhita quipped.

Ignatius had never liked Josiah. He believed him to be overly driven and generally dangerous, which was ludicrous to Bakhita since Josiah was the most rule-following man she'd ever met.

"No, I'm here to check on you," Ignatius answered with concern.

Ignatius was not close to his sister; he considered her prideful and harsh. Still, she was his sister, and at this moment, when the man she loved—whether she'd admit it or not—was marrying another, he felt bad for her. Ignatius didn't blame Josiah. He would've married Amelia in a second if she'd given him a chance. For some unknown reason she only had eyes for Josiah. How such a selfish jerk won a woman as beautiful and good as Amelia, Ignatius would never understand. Maybe Josiah was a better man than he realized, or maybe—and this was more likely—Josiah was simply a better liar than he realized and Amelia had no idea who he really was.

"Since when have you ever checked on me?" Bakhita said in a tone of irritation she used when speaking to her brother.

"To be fair, you're the big sister and I'm the little brother. You're the one who's supposed to look out for me," he said with a grin that emphasized the dimples in his cheeks.

Bakhita laughed. "Please, I'm barely eleven months older, and you have six inches and a hundred pounds of muscle more than me. It's not fair."

"Life isn't fair," Ignatius answered, settling onto the dirt beside his sister.

"For now," she said.

"Ah, still focused on making everyone the same?" Ignatius said, wishing his sister was not so scary.

"Not the same. You know how many eye and hair color alterations my team has already created."

"Right. We can all look different, we can even look like peacocks if we want, but on the inside no one will be any different from anyone else."

"No one will be *better* than anyone else."

"I have to tell you, sis, it's a boring world you and Josiah are trying to create."

That was a lie. He found their version of the future far from boring. It was terrifying, but to tell her would only fuel her desire to create it.

"How is it boring to ensure everyone has the same abilities and opportunities to pursue them? My work will practically guarantee a person has a happy life, at least much happier than now."

"You can't guarantee happiness," Ignatius replied.

"I'm not so sure. It was Josiah who helped me think it through," Bakhita said with a mixture of pain for Josiah's recent choices and pride at all they'd accomplished together.

"Think what through?" Ignatius asked, unable to ignore the growing knot in his stomach.

She crossed her legs and turned toward him. "What are the aspects of a person that lead to the greatest degree of unhappiness for that person and society as a whole?"

"Indigestion? Poor sleep? I have no idea."

"Of course you don't," Bakhita said in a superior tone. "Unhappiness—or most of it—happens when people don't follow the rules of society. When people act in illogical ways and break the rules, the world starts to fall apart."

"You can't make people follow rules, Bakhita. We were given free will. It's part of what makes us human. We choose our own paths, we aren't robots," Ignatius said, feeling more uneasy.

"True, but wouldn't it be great if we were?"

"Wouldn't it be great if people were mindless zombie robots? No, I don't think so," he said.

She giggled. "Not mindless zombie robots, silly, perfectly intelligent people who follow the rules." Her eyes were gleaming up at him.

A shiver ran through Ignatius's body. He whispered, "Have you created an alteration to make people do whatever they're told?"

She leaned back, placing her hands on the dirt behind her, her eyes transfixed on the church. "Not yet, but I'm close," she said, sounding disappointed. "Thankfully, Josiah's work is further along than mine … though even he will tell you his work is easier. Still, it's a lot to be proud of. His artificial womb, or gestation machine, as everyone around the lab is calling it, worked. Our first human, gestated from a machine, came into full existence three days ago."

"The gestation machine is operational?" Ignatius's throat was going dry.

"Why do you say it like that? You know how much freedom this gives everyone. Never again will a child be killed simply when the woman carrying it doesn't want it."

Ignatius swallowed hard. "Yes, that is a good thing, a very good thing. A child killed because it had the misfortune of being conceived by a woman who didn't want it has always upset me. It's so wasteful. But I've never been comfortable with your lab owning such a machine."

Bakhita scoffed, saying, "So you aren't upset about the technology existing, only that I have access to it."

"Not only you … you and Josiah make a dangerous pair. I have a bad feeling about this and I always have."

"That's the problem, little brother. You and your feelings. You're too much like Mom and Dad to even partially understand what Josiah and I are working on. Science isn't about feelings, it's about reason. It shouldn't be tied to outdated notions and concepts. It needs to move forward in a purely systematic way."

"You mean without ethics or morals to guide it?" he said. He felt the perspiration starting to drip from his forehead.

"Ethics and morals are not objective. They're defined by the person defining them."

"In your opinion," Ignatius answered. He and his sister had had this conversation so many times, he felt no need to say more.

"In everyone's opinion. It's a moot point, Ignatius. Everything we do is ethical. How could it not be? We're working nonstop to make the world better, safer, fairer. Do you know how many genetic disorders have already been eliminated through my work and the work of others?"

"A lot?" Ignatius answered, doing what he could to keep his voice calm.

In a mocking tone, Bakhita stated, "Yeah, a whole lot."

"Aren't you even a little concerned about what will happen once people are grown in a machine instead of an actual womb? Who will that child belong to?"

Bakhita cringed at the word *womb*. It was an outdated word she had never cared for. It was the reason she had coined the term *gestation machine*.

"First of all, people are not grown. They're not a tomato plant. They're gestated. And Josiah is working with legislatures to establish appropriate laws surrounding children who are gestated from his machine and the many more machines sure to follow."

"*He's* working with legislatures?"

"Yes, there must be laws about what constitutes a person— which might be different from a human. It's unclear at this moment. It's something Josiah is playing with."

"Have you lost your mind!" Ignatius exclaimed, no longer able to hide his emotions. "Look at your skin, look at mine. Don't you get what you're doing?"

She held up her left arm and admired her perfectly smooth skin with its golden mahogany coloring. "What're you talking about?"

"Two hundred years ago, people whose skin was our color were slaves, and now you, a black woman, are helping to create an entirely new race of slaves. You can't do that!"

"It's ironic you asked me if I've lost my mind, when clearly you've lost yours. We aren't creating slaves, and since when has skin color mattered?"

"It used to matter a lot, just like it's going to matter when a kid is born to a machine."

"A child can't be born from a machine, it can be gestated, and it has been."

"And you don't think that matters?" he said, his voice rising in pitch.

"No offense, but you're not making sense," Bakhita said in a dismissive tone.

"Bakhita, who *owns* the child that was *born* three days ago?"

"I told you he was *gestated*," she responded flatly. "And you know people don't own people."

He rubbed his hands through his short hair in utter frustration. "Where is the child?"

"At the lab, being cared for by one of the technicians."

"A technician?" he said, appalled at his sister.

"A competent one—actually, several. Trust me, all his needs are being met perfectly."

"What about love? That is a need, isn't it? Who is loving the child? Who is going to rock it to sleep and care for it and hold it when it cries and make it feel treasured—not just now, but in five, ten, fifteen years. Who will be the child's family?"

She said calmly, "That is what Josiah is figuring out."

Ignatius felt panic and anger, clearly seeing what his sister was not able to even conceive of. "*Josiah* is not the one to *figure this out*. Josiah doesn't have a moral bone in his body, and frankly, neither do you. You are creating *people*, not a lab experiment. The little boy that was *born* needs a *family*, not technicians. He needs to be loved and protected."

She felt a slight vibration from the band she wore on her left wrist. Bakhita flipped her wrist toward herself. The screen lit up with a message, and she exhaled with disappointment. "You can relax," she said. "The infant passed away. His lungs were not developed enough. Obviously, Josiah has more work to do on the gestation machine."

Ignatius felt as though he'd been shot through the heart. "Bakhita, he was a living human being and you're speaking of him as if he was nothing more than a failed experiment."

"Experimenting is how *real* science progresses. And yes, sometimes those experiments fail and those failures guide us. Josiah will learn a great deal from the autopsy he will conduct on that infant. Perhaps there's an alteration I could create to make a child better able to withstand the conditions of a gestation machine," she said, already thinking of what to do differently next time.

"You have to stop," Ignatius demanded.

Bakhita's big brown eyes stared at him. "Stop what?"

"Every bit of it. The artificial womb, the genetic alterations. It has to stop."

She stood. "You truly have lost your senses," she said, brushing the dirt from her jeans.

He was on his feet beside her. Forcing his voice to be steady, he said, "Bakhita, you are playing God and that is a very dangerous thing to do."

She laughed and said, "And since when have you believed in God?"

"Since right now," he said, jabbing an index finger toward the ground. "I never saw the world so clearly as I do right now. You have to stop. You have to undo what you've done."

"We're making the world *better*. You might be too simple to understand, but it's the truth."

"That might be your intent. I can give you that, but it is not what you're doing. You can't mess around with free will, or intelligence, or even eye color—you have to stop. And Josiah's machine …." Ignatius ran his fingers across his hair. "Those kids you're creating without thinking about it, the embryos you've destroyed in your so-called experiments, those souls are real. There will be consequences. What you're doing is going to have awful consequences that not even I can predict."

"Ha! You can't predict anything. You can't even understand the possibilities of what we're creating."

He stood taller, his chest broadening as he stepped closer to his sister. His voice was low and deep. "It is *you* who can't understand what you're doing. It is *you* who will be held responsible. May God have mercy on your soul."

From across the meadow of flowering weeds, the bells of the church rang and the oversized wooden doors swung open. The guests started to come out. In the midst of them, a tall, fair-skinned man in a tuxedo escorted a beaming woman dressed in a flowing white gown.

At the sight of them, Bakhita's body stiffened with jealousy.

Beside her, Ignatius felt dizzy, as though the world was swirling too fast. He rubbed his temples to fight the start of a headache. He watched Josiah escort Amelia down the long brick path which meandered to a well-manicured area of trees. Focusing on Amelia, Ignatius became both calmer and more panicked. She'd always had a calming effect on him, but to see her with Josiah …. Amelia was carrying her bouquet of flowers and Josiah was obediently holding up the expansive train of his wife's gown, down the path, toward the trees. Ignatius yearned to call out to Amelia, to somehow get her to undo what she had just done. But he remained stuck, frozen in time, unable to act, unable to stop the inevitable.

***

The young bride knew little of her husband's true self. She saw only the good in him, which meant she saw a small portion of who he was. If she'd been less naïve, she would've seen the truth—or more of it. This was one of the drawbacks of being raised in such a loving way: she'd never learned to recognize a liar. She'd learn the truth soon enough, but in this moment she believed her husband every bit the hero he believed himself to be.

Amelia was proud of his work. He was creating an artificial womb with the potential to save hundreds of thousands, if not millions, of lives. To her mind, there could be no more heroic work. Only three days ago a precious baby boy had been born from his machine. A beautiful child who had a chance at life when none had existed before. In her mind and her husband's, his work was noble and life-giving. The womb would save preterm infants and countless more whose biological mothers didn't want them. His work was one of the many reasons she loved him.

Just as she knew very little about the core of her husband, she knew even less about his work. She knew nothing of the hundreds of millions of embryos at his disposal, or the genetic alterations his business partner was working on, or his work with legislatures to define what a person was. Had she known any of these things, she wouldn't have married him or even spoken to him again. She would've recognized him for who he was and his work for what it was—dangerous and without any concept of morality. She knew none of this.

As Ignatius had said, Amelia was too good for Josiah. She who was without vice couldn't recognize it in others. In this way, perhaps she was dim-witted, as Bakhita believed. After all, she took the words of her husband at face value. If she had a flaw, this was it: too trusting, too good.

Below the canopy of trees the young couple followed the brick path away from the church, toward an even older structure. The building centered among the trees was called a shrine and it housed a statue of a woman nursing her infant son. This sculpture was known as the Nursing Madonna, a holdover from the most ancient days of Christianity. To many, including Josiah and Bakhita, this place was the embodiment of magical thinking which only the most simpleminded fools engaged in. To Amelia it was a place where heaven kissed the earth and the mother of her Lord interceded with her son for those who wanted a child … which Amelia very much wanted.

The glowing young bride lovingly placed her bouquet at the feet of the nursing mother. Amelia turned and gazed adoringly up at her husband, who wrapped his strong arms around her.

"Our life together is going to be so beautiful," she said as she nuzzled against his chest.

Josiah Northup tightened his arms around his wife and murmured, "The most beautiful."

Perseverance

Amelia sat at the piano, the only thing left in the forgotten church. Forgotten by everyone except her. Her fingers flowed across the keys as if the music had a life of its own, which she shared. The two worked in unison to create beauty. Her eyes were closed, but she heard his footsteps. They were angry … they were often angry. A tear slipped down her cheek. She had prayed so dearly for a beautiful life, a life of music and children, for a good and true husband, a man who'd put his faith and family above everything else.

She did not have a beautiful life. She hated to think such an awful thought; it felt so ungrateful. It was her reality, though. Her life was nothing like she'd hoped and prayed and worked for—not at all the life she'd wanted.

How had she been so wrong? she'd asked herself over and over. She knew she shouldn't ask such things and should accept the life she had, not spending her time lost in what could've been. Even in the best moments, when she held her young son as he drifted off to sleep, she still could not comprehend how she had been so wrong about his father.

She had been beautiful once. She still was, though she no longer thought of such things. So many young men had wanted her for their own. Many spoke only of partnering. She was made for more. She was made for marriage. There had been another; Bakhita's brother, Ignatius, would have gladly married her. But to be related to Bakhita in any way … heat rose to Amelia's cheeks. If she had married Ignatius, she at least would not have had to worry about Bakhita as competition.

19

"Bakhita said you were here," Josiah shouted across the empty church.

Amelia did not stop playing. The music continued in her; it kept her alive and she kept it alive, no matter how much he struggled to destroy them both.

"I'm talking to you," he said as he neared the piano.

She took a deep breath and finished playing the song flowing from her as if she were the mighty St. Johns, the river she had grown up next to, the river she loved.

"No, you are talking *at* me. There is a difference," she said, gently lifting her fingers from the keys.

"Why are you here?" he said. "You know renovation begins today."

"As you often remind me, Josiah, you're a brilliant man, so you must have realized that is exactly why I am here. And let us be clear, it is not *renovation*, it is *destruction*." Amelia stared up into his cold eyes—which had once beheld her with such kindness.

She had not seen kindness from him for so long. How long? she wondered. It had gradually withered after they married. Each year, the man she had fallen in love with had faded. And now the man who stood before her barely resembled the man she'd promised to share her life with. How had everything changed so fast?

"Where is Joshua?" Josiah asked, his tone accusatory.

"With my mother," Amelia answered placidly.

"Your mother is past the age of uselessness," he said.

"You know I hate that term."

"That's the term for those of her age."

"It's the name you and your politician friends created," she said sharply.

Josiah didn't respond. She was right, and he was not ashamed of his accomplishments. He had done a lot of work to make the world better. Nevertheless, his wife acknowledged none of it. How he had ever thought he could be happy with her …. Why was he still with her? It was a question he often asked himself.

Amelia did not believe in divorce, but he certainly had no objection to it. Given that her presence had no bearing on his behavior, he had found no reason to go through the paperwork of divorce. Besides, he liked his son living full-time under his roof. Though the main reason Josiah stayed was because leaving would, on some level, be admitting he had failed or, at least, made a mistake, and neither was acceptable for Josiah Northup.

"Come on, I'll drive you home," he said.

"How could you?" Tears of sorrow and rage streamed down her face.

"How could I what?" he said, thinking how right Bakhita was. Amelia was overly dramatic.

In reality, Amelia was calm to a degree her husband could not fathom.

"How could you destroy this place, of all places? How could you desecrate the most sacred with the most vile?"

"*Vile?* Why is it the one person on the planet who can't understand how world changing my work is, is my wife?"

"Oh, it's world changing, in the darkest of ways," she said, crossing her arms.

"You're a sentimental fool, just like your parents," he said.

"We were married here," she said, standing and gesturing to where the altar had stood. "That means nothing to you?"

They both knew it didn't.

"Isn't it better for the building to be used for something useful instead of sitting empty?" he said, trying to reason with her. He had work to do, and this conversation had already taken too much time.

"Useful? Why is everything about how useful someone or something is? Why does beauty mean nothing to you?"

He groaned. "Beauty, always beauty. Beauty is useless, it doesn't matter!"

Ironically, Amelia's beauty had first drawn him to her. In his defense, he had not married her solely for that reason. She was kind and he liked her smile, and so many other men—especially that fool, Ignatius—had wanted her for their own. Obviously, she was valuable, the most valuable, and so he deserved her.

Josiah would advise his son to be wiser. There was no need to marry, and if he did want to partner, he needed to do a better job at selecting a woman. Josiah would help him. His son would have an easier life than him, the sort of life Josiah should've had. Joshua's partner would be supportive and encouraging.

She'd give him the kind of attention Amelia no longer gave Josiah. That was another thing. He'd strongly encourage his son not to reproduce or even select a child. There was no need. Not that children did not occasionally enrich life, but why be so burdened? And with the vast number of embryos and the work he and Bakhita were doing, there was no reason for couples to conceive or even raise a child.

Amelia's soft words broke into his thoughts: "Josiah …? It matters to me."

He felt a slight twinge of pain in his chest. Had he been unkind by convincing his friends in the government to give him this old church? Had he been motivated to hurt his wife, as Ignatius had accused him? No, Ignatius was an idiot who understood nothing. At least Josiah had saved Amelia from a fool like him. Yes, she made his life more difficult than it should be. Still, he did care about her.

He stepped forward. "I'm sorry," he said. "The world is changing for the better, like this place is changing for the better. You and I can't stand in the way. If I didn't get this building, someone else would have."

"Any other purpose would be better," she said with quiet rage.

His face contorted. "You like to talk about sin. There are far more sinful things than creating life. You used to be proud of the work I was doing."

"That's because I believed you when you said you were working on an artificial *womb*."

"That is exactly what I created," he said, frustrated by his wife's continued lack of understanding.

"No, you created a *gestation machine*. Call it what it really is! You never intended to save children whose mothers didn't want them. You intended to create slaves."

"Gestates are not slaves," he said mechanically, as if he'd pronounced the line a hundred times before.

She stepped toward him. "We both know they will be," she said in a lower voice. "It's why you want this place, a place to *raise* them, to *train* them is the real word."

"Children must be cared for," he said, as if his wife was too foolish to understand.

"Yes, dear, they must be cared for, as I am well aware, given that *I* am the one who cares for *our* son. And he is cared for, he is *loved*. The children you are creating … who is loving them? You and Bakhita and your teams? At best, you're experimenting on them, but we both know it is worse than that."

"We're learning how best to care for them and collecting data as we go. We're scientists and that's what scientists do." Josiah felt beyond irritated at the irrationality of his wife.

She said, "Children should live with families who love them, not in a giant science experiment with people who have the compassion of lab rats."

He'd had enough. "Since we're turning your church into our science lab, perhaps your imaginary God will protect them. You're welcome to pray about it from our home, because you will never set foot on this property again." He grasped her roughly by the arm and led her, squirming, down the center aisle of the nave.

She wrestled free. He grabbed her and lifted her onto his shoulder. She shrieked in anger, but stopped fighting. He had always prided himself on being in top physical condition without the help of alterations—not that he'd anticipated using his strength to carry his wife. How strange it was … the last time they'd walked down this path, she had been beaming up at him and he had been convinced she was the most beautiful woman in the region.

He kicked open the door, and the construction workers were there waiting, with Bakhita by their side. The workers dropped their gaze while Bakhita appeared horrified. She hated violence. She was the reason guns were no longer allowed in the region. Josiah had done that for her. Now he looked like a Neanderthal in front of her.

"She wasn't being reasonable," he explained as he put Amelia down.

"You're destroying something good and true and beautiful," Amelia said, angry and calm at the same time. "May God have mercy on your souls, each of you," she said, scowling at her husband, Bakhita, and the construction workers.

Bakhita and Josiah locked eyes and laughed to themselves.

Two of the construction workers who observed this looked at one another, and turned and walked away. The others watched them leave. Some seemed to be debating if they should stay or go. No others left.

Amelia glared at her husband and at that moment an intense change took place within her. The anger threatening to consume her left, and in its place she felt sorrow—a true, deep sorrow not for her loss, which was great, but for her husband's soul.

"God forgive them, they know not what they do," she said softly, and walked away from her church for the last time.

As she moved among the trees beyond the yard of what was once her church, she stepped lightly upon the bricks that led to what had been the shrine.

The heavy oak door of the ancient shrine opened slowly; she forced it open, straining against its weight. She thought of how quickly the hinges had rusted in the Florida weather, without maintenance. It was the same as our souls without the sacraments. A tear slipped down her cheek.

She had come here often as a child, with her parents and other families. Amelia had many friends when she was young. She never felt alone in her faith or in her life. She blinked away the tears as she sat on the dirty concrete floor where a kneeler had once rested. She gazed up at where the altar had been. The world she'd been born into was so different than the world her son had entered. She supposed every mother could say the same, yet something about these times felt unique … extreme.

Jesus's words from the cross and David's words from the psalm escaped her lips: "My God, my God, why have you abandoned me?"

As she breathed slowly to calm herself, the scent of roses infused the empty building. She lowered her head into her hands and wept.

Contrition

Amelia knelt on the dirt covering the cracked concrete floor. She sat back against her heels, the toes of her sneakers bent. Her hands were pressed together and her gaze was fixed on a spot in the ancient wall. The recess had held something; it was now empty. The emptiness did not stop her from seeing what had been there for close to three centuries. In her memory, a small statue of a woman nursing a baby boy remained in the alcove.

This image often appeared in her mind. It evoked mixed feelings of peace and sorrow. She couldn't think of it without being reminded of the life she so deeply longed for but would never have.

She had made the decision many years ago to offer her life for all those who had no idea the pain they were causing, most specifically her husband and those he worked with. This offering was a sort of silent martyrdom. It was both sacrificial and self-serving. It was the only way she could bring any sort of sense to her own life.

"Amelia?" The voice was soft.

Amelia whirled. She had not expected anyone. The dappled sunlight coming through the opening where the door had once stood made it hard to distinguish who was there. Her eyes adjusted, and she thought she must be seeing wrong.

"Bakhita," she said, embarrassed that of all the people who could've found her in this place of raw vulnerability, it would be the one closest to her husband.

Bakhita glanced from Amelia to the empty alcove and back. Amelia felt the sting of judgment. She had been labeled long ago as the crazy one. It shouldn't hurt being thought of that way by someone she had no respect for, but it did.

"The guards said they saw a woman come down here."

"This is public land. I'm allowed to be here," Amelia stated as she rose and brushed the dirt from her long skirt.

Cautiously, Bakhita stepped closer to her. "You're not in trouble. That's not why I'm here."

"Why are you here?" Amelia said defiantly. "You're far above this deserted place … above me. You could've sent the guards to tell me to leave, or told Josiah. He couldn't stop me from coming, though he'd try."

If Amelia had not been so caught off guard, she would've noticed the change in Bakhita. There was almost, though not quite, humility in her expression and a nervousness in her body.

Bakhita said, "I've wanted to talk to you for some time, but didn't know how to do it. So when the guards told me they saw someone down here, I hoped it was you."

Amelia had no response. If Bakhita had spoken with cruelty, Amelia would've understood the intent—she'd use her presence here against her. It would be one more indication of how out of touch with reality Amelia was, one more reason why Josiah should leave her. Not that Amelia would've minded. She had decided long ago she'd never leave him. Yet in numerous moments she had prayed he'd leave her so she could be free of him—as free as she could be of the father of her son.

32

But Bakhita had spoken to her with kindness, something she had not done since long before Amelia was married, and to this, Amelia had no understanding.

"I ... I don't know how to say this," Bakhita said, clearly troubled.

Now Amelia understood. "There is no need to say anything," Amelia said, standing taller. "You're a fool if you think he'll be faithful."

The words stung Bakhita, though she didn't know why. Amelia was right; Josiah had not attempted or intended to keep his wedding vows.

"No, I don't suppose he'd ever be faithful to anyone. Not to you and not to me," Bakhita said, acknowledging, at least to herself, the role she had played in hurting Amelia through the years.

"Then why do you want him?" Amelia asked, studying Bakhita.

"I don't," Bakhita said.

"You're lying," Amelia whispered with dangerous boldness. No one was more powerful than Bakhita except Josiah.

Bakhita slumped forward as a small groan came from her throat. She raised her head. Her eyes showed what might be considered by some as contrition.

"There was a time when I did want Josiah for my own, and during that time ... I am sorry," she said, staring at Amelia as if trying to will Amelia to see her soul. "I am eternally sorry. I've been so wrong about so many things and I don't know how to make it right."

"I-I am confused," Amelia said, glancing up into the corners of the building and down at Bakhita's arms. No cameras, no wristband.

Bakhita whispered, "What I've created, what Josiah and I created … we shouldn't have."

Amelia took a step back. "If you're trying to trap me, you should've chosen a better location. There are no cameras here," she said cautiously, now wondering if others were listening outside of the building.

"I'm not," Bakhita said, and took two steps toward her. "I'm not trying to trap you. It's the reason I'm here. This is one of the few places in the region where we can speak privately. You must know it's safe, or you wouldn't come here."

"You know I come here?" Amelia asked with a slight tremble. If Bakhita knew, so did Josiah.

"Josiah told me years ago. He tracks your car," Bakhita told her, partially in warning.

Amelia wrapped her arms around her body, the air suddenly feeling icy. "I should've realized he knew I came here. For some reason I … I guess since he never confronted me about it … I thought I was safe here," Amelia said, her white skin turning paler.

"You aren't safe anywhere," Bakhita said. Her voice was not threatening; it was apologetic.

"No, I'm not," Amelia said, moving toward the opening in the wall where the door had once been.

It was time for her to leave this place. Maybe someday she could return, but she had underestimated how carefully her husband followed every step she took. She supposed she should be grateful he had not ordered the government to destroy this building, like he had destroyed her church.

Bakhita called out, "Please don't leave."

"I need to be getting home," Amelia replied. She was sure there were no cameras in her house; Josiah did not allow them.

She knew he wished he had them so he could monitor her and the kids in his absence, but he was smart enough to realize that if he could monitor the system, others could tap into it. At least she was safe in her home and could raise her son and Carolyn the way she saw fit when he wasn't around, which, thankfully, was most of the time.

Bakhita blurted out, "I need your help."

Amelia turned to her. "What can I possibly do for you?"

"Help me fix it," she begged.

"Help you fix what?"

"Everything I've done, help me undo it."

Amelia turned her head to the side in confusion.

"Everything—the alterations, the borns, the gestates … I never … I never should have …." Bakhita stopped, unable to say the words.

Amelia said, "Experimented with babies and turned them into slaves?"

Bakhita dropped her head forward into her right hand. When Bakhita's curls moved, Amelia saw streaks of gray in the dark hair. More than a decade ago Bakhita had created an alteration which severely slowed the aging process. Amelia had not received that alteration, or any alteration, and so her own brown hair had streaks of gray. But Bakhita … why would she have signs of aging?

"I didn't understand what I was doing," Bakhita said, looking up.

Amelia noticed thin lines etched into the skin around Bakhita's eyes.

Bakhita said, "You did, and Ignatius did. I didn't. I should've, but I was so focused on trying to create the alterations and proving Josiah's gestation machine would work, I never thought about what would happen to the kids we created." She clenched her fists and shook her thick curls. "No, that's a lie. I didn't care what happened to them. They were there to be studied, nothing more." She wrung her hands in a frantic burst of energy. "What've I done?"

"Your hair is graying," Amelia said, trying to understand what she was witnessing.

Bakhita exhaled loudly and held the back of her neck with her hands. "I've undone the alterations I did to myself."

Amelia studied her. Bakhita's body was changing with age in the same way as her own.

"Why would you undo them?" Amelia asked.

"I want nothing to do with what I've created," Bakhita said, anxious for Amelia to understand her, to help her. Somehow, someway, she must set right everything she'd done wrong.

Amelia stared. "You're serious," she said, cocking her head.

"Help me, please, help me fix it," Bakhita begged, stepping closer to Amelia.

"An awakening of conscience," Amelia said in awe. "It must be the Holy Spirit. How else could anyone ever explain this? It's like Paul on his way to Damascus."

Bakhita had not heard such words since childhood, yet she understood the reference. It felt as if her heart was being stabbed—not in a literal sense, there was no physical pain—but the emotion of the moment, of the awareness Amelia's words brought her were nearly too much to bear. In that instant Bakhita understood she had been wrong, not only about her work and the children she had created, but about all of it. Had it been true, the stories her parents had told her, the stories Amelia believed? Had Bakhita been wrong about every single aspect of her life?

"Why? What brought about such a … a change?" Amelia asked, starting to believe Bakhita might feel some remorse at destroying the world.

Tears began to sting Bakhita's eyes. She was feeling too much at the memory of the child—a memory she should not have had. She shouldn't have been there, and the child, especially that child, the sweetest gestate she'd ever created … the pain of it was breaking her to her core … that child never should've died.

In a gesture of compassion, Amelia stepped closer to Bakhita, but as Amelia was about to embrace her, they heard the sound of someone approaching. She moved backward as her husband stepped onto the fallen door and entered the building.

Josiah's expression changed from frustration to anger, and next, to confusion. "I didn't expect to find you two together," he said.

Bakhita's posture changed. She quickly brushed the tears from her eyes and stood taller. "The guards told me a woman was here. I assumed it was Amelia. I wanted to save you the embarrassment, so I came before anyone else."

"Is that why you're crying?" Josiah asked, puzzled. This was one more example of how strange Bakhita had been acting ever since the young female gestate was accidentally beaten to death in front of her.

"It's an allergic reaction to the mold growing in the corners of this old building," Bakhita said, feigning irritation as she pointed to the corner where a patch of black fuzzy stuff grew near the roof.

"I thought you were altered against allergies," he said. Josiah also noticed the streaks of gray in her hair.

"Apparently not against mold," she said in a way that made him feel foolish for asking.

"Of course," he said. "My apologies for confusing you for my overly dramatic wife," Josiah said, tipping his head slightly at her.

"Amelia, don't you think you should be getting home?" His tone was not kind, but not cruel either. It was indifferent, condescending.

"Yes, I should," she said, not wanting to be in her husband's presence any longer than necessary.

She started for the exit. Josiah moved out of the way to allow her to pass.

"I'm … I'm sorry we did not get to finish our conversation," Bakhita said to Amelia.

Josiah stared at Bakhita. Never had she been kind to Amelia, not since his marriage more than twenty years earlier.

Amelia's fingers grazed the splintered doorframe. She turned and made eye contact with Bakhita. "I come here because it's where I remember how things used to be, and it's where I pray. But I can pray anywhere. It doesn't have to be here, so I won't come here anymore. Our Lord and his mother will understand. They always understand. Our Lord never forsakes us, no matter how hopeless a cause might appear. And no matter what I've done, I know he always loves me and forgives me. Even if I'd destroyed the world, he would still love me and in prayer would guide me. And though my own mother has passed on and I miss her dearly, I find a great deal of comfort knowing our Lord gave us his mother. So I still have a mother who is always loving me and guiding me, if I allow her."

"Why are you saying such nonsense?" Josiah asked with disdain at the ridiculous way his wife was speaking.

Amelia met his gaze and said, "I don't know, dear, sometimes I just say things out loud. Maybe I wanted to explain why I wouldn't be here any longer. I will miss this holy of holy places. It seems a better place than most to talk to the Lord. Of course the best was at Mass, but you have outlawed such ancient rituals," she stated, blinking up at her husband.

"All communal religious practices were outlawed. It was not specific to yours," he stated cooly. "You and everyone else are welcome to practice their religious beliefs from their own home."

"Yes, that is kind of your government friends to allow, and you do allow me to pray at home, which is also kind," she said in an indifferent tone. "Of course I am not a priest, and so I am not able to fully practice my faith. I suppose I should be grateful for what you do allow."

He was startled not by his wife's words; she had said them many times before. The emotionless way she spoke struck him. She was placating him—he understood this—and he didn't know how to respond.

Amelia released her hand from the doorframe and stepped out of the shrine. A wave of sorrow engulfed her. This would be the last time she'd set foot in this once holy place. It was no longer safe for her to enter now that she understood how closely she was monitored. The world was changing too fast, and with it her husband's power and influence were growing too vast. As she stepped from the shrine she heard Josiah's voice.

"She's such a strange woman, such a constant embarrassment," he said to Bakhita.

"She's wiser than you think," Bakhita answered.

Instinctively, Amelia followed the brick path that had long ago been buried by soil and rotting leaves. It was the path she'd taken since before she could walk. Then it was her parents who carried her along the path between their church and the ancient shrine. She had carried her own infant son along the same path, but Josiah allowed her to do this only once, when Joshua was first born. This was a source of great sadness for Amelia, who had wished she could share this part of her life with her son. She sniffed at the sorrow she felt and inhaled the scent of damp leaves, a smell representing both death and rebirth. The warm breeze blew, tousling the ends of Amelia's hair. The wind carried another smell, the faintest scent of roses. In that moment she felt something she had not felt in a long time. It took her another moment to recognize it.

"Hope," she whispered to herself as she raised her gaze to the barbed wire encircling the gestation firm—the place that had once been her church.

"The pendulum is swinging," she said softly as she veered from the hidden path toward her car at the far side of the meadow. "The pendulum is swinging."

If you enjoyed *The Hope of Sorrows: Short Stories of the Altered Series*, please consider sharing your copy with a friend and leaving a review.

Please visit the author at www.Jacqueline-Brown.com for updates, special offers, and new releases.

Made in the USA
Middletown, DE
04 December 2025

24009048R00031